For T. L., who taught me to love reading
A. H.

For my Mom
J. J M.

Text copyright © 2004 by Amy Hest
Illustrations copyright © 2004 by Jon J Muth

First edition 2004

Library of Congress Cataloging-in-Publication Data
Hest, Amy.
Mr. George Baker / Amy Hest ; illustrated by Jon J Muth. — 1st ed. 2004
p. cm.
Summary: Harry sits on the porch with Mr. George Baker, an African American who is
one hundred years old but can still dance and play the drums, waiting for the school bus
that will take them both to the class where they are learning to read.
ISBN 0-7636-1233-2
[1. Literacy — Fiction. 2. Old age — Fiction. 3. Friendship — Fiction. 4. African Americans — Fiction.]
I. Muth, Jon J, ill. II. Title.
PZ7.H4375Mr2004
[E] — dc21   2002074136

4 6 8 10 9 7 5

Printed in China

This book was typeset in Integrity.
The illustrations were done in watercolor.

Candlewick Press
2067 Massachusetts Avenue
Cambridge, Massachusetts 02140

visit us at www.candlewick.com

Mr. George Baker

Amy Hest

illustrated by Jon J Muth

CANDLEWICK PRESS
CAMBRIDGE, MASSACHUSETTS

See this man?
This one here, sitting on the porch?

That's Mr. George Baker,
and he's a *hundred* years old,
no kidding.

"Hurry up, Harry! Mr. Harry-in-Charge."
That's George, all snappy and happy in the morning.
He always calls "Hurry up, Harry"
when I'm crossing lawns — his and mine — and
he's always there first, waiting on the porch.

See his pants, all baggy, baggy, baggy?
What holds them up — suspenders!
Brown baggy pants with two side pockets,
and two in back.
There's candy in those pockets.
Little chocolate candies in twisty silver wrappers.
George pops one in his mouth and I do too.

We wait on the porch and chew.

I like his crumpled hat
and his long stretchy legs.
His shoes are crumpled too,
with long shoelaces.
Mine always come undone in the morning.
"Let's have a look," says George,
making two double knots
that never come undone,
not ever.

See this man?
This one here,
zipping up his book bag?
His book bag is red like mine,
and there's a book inside.

But George can't read.
A hundred years old, and he never learned how.
"That must be corrected," says George.

I really like his sweater,
all hangy with three buttons.
It's chilly in the morning, and
we both hug our knees.
And wait. We wait, watching
leaves blow off trees.

They fly for a while; they float.
They tumble for a while; they swoop.

Now the screen door creaks,
and you know who teeters out?
Mrs. Baker, and some people say she's ninety!
"Well, here you are, Harry, looking after my George."
Mrs. Baker puts a sack on the step beside George,
and there's lunch in the sack for later.

"For the man I love,"
says Mrs. Baker.

"Why Mrs. B! You flatter me!"
George gets up, all crookedy and slow,
and the next thing you know,
they're dancing!

Then Mrs. Baker gives a wave and a wink. "Goodbye," she says. "Be good," she says, and goes back in the house with purple shutters.

George Baker and me, George Baker and *I*,
we sit on the step and wait.

Side by side, we wait.

See these crookedy fingers,
going *tappidy* on his knees?
They fly across his knees.
    Tappidy-boom.
        Tappidy-boom.
    Tappidy-boom-boom-tap.
George Baker is a drummer man, and
some people say he's famous.

Sometimes he drums on
his porch at night,
and the neighbors come by.
Up the road and down the road,
they come to hear my drummer man.

13

"Shh, listen!"
George gets up, real slow.
I take his hand and he takes mine
and we shuffle down the walk
to the big school bus.

"Morning," says the driver.
"We've been waiting," answers George.

There are twenty-two kids
on the bus plus four grownups
on the bus. They all want George.

"Over here!" they cry. "Sit here!" they say,
but George sits with me. Each and every day.

See this man? This one in Room 7?
That's Mr. George Baker,
and he's a hundred years old, no kidding.

16

He's learning to read with the grownups in Room 7, and my room is right down the hall. I'm learning, too, and it's hard.

"We can do it," says George after school.
Our books are green, and his lips
sound out the letters.
Real slow. But his fingers fly across
his knees. Like a big old drum.

Tappidy-boom.
Tappidy-boom.
Tappidy-boom-boom-tap.

18